Winston

Winston

The Adventures of a Brave
Australian Rainbow Lorikeet

DANNIE J TAYLOR

To order additional copies of this book, contact:
Xlibris
AU TFN: 1 800 844 927 (Toll Free inside Australia)
AU Local: 0283 108 187 (+61 2 8310 8187 from outside Australia)
www.Xlibris.com.au
Orders@Xlibris.com.au
825598

I dedicate this novella to those who have suffered a stroke, and to the people who care for them.
Thank You!

ACKNOWLEDGEMENT

I thank Jeanne Godfrey, my wife, for not only her typing skills, and constructive comments, but also her infinite patience.

FOREWORD

Despite its size this novella took a long time to write. Three years ago my eleven year old grandson, who enjoys hearing my tall stories, suggested I should write about our rainbow lorikeets, which we have owned for many years. Instead of writing about our own rainbow lorikeets I decided to write an adventure come educational story about the exploits of a male rainbow lorikeet. Shortly after starting this project I suffered a stroke that not only landed me in the hospital for some time, but also took away a large chunk of my memory and the ability to speak, which was a frightening experience. I knew what needed to be said but the brain refused to transfer it to the vocals. After many months of therapy my faculties gradually returned. But another problem arose. Before the stroke I had written the acclaimed novel, High Seas Cowboy, and several published short stories.

But post stroke I found it almost impossible to string together a seven-word sentence that made any sense, and this remained for almost two years. During this time, I had to teach myself how to write again. When this was accomplished, I returned to the rainbow lorikeet story. Today they are one of the most popular pet birds in the world. This story is meant for all ages and it is based on my knowledge about them through having many as pets and observing them in the wild for over thirty years.

DANNIE TAYLOR

CHAPTER ONE

This story is about a brave little rainbow lorikeet named Winston. He is on the front cover of this book. As you can see, all the vivid colours of the rainbow are displayed in his feathers, hence the name of his species, and yet despite these brilliant colours, they are difficult to see when in the tree canopies. But if you listen though, they are impossible to miss as they boisterously climb through the trees, foraging for their favourite food, the nectar within the eucalyptus flowers, or tussling with their flock mates.

Although, Winston never enjoyed any of these activities, because he was bred in captivity by a professional rainbow lorikeet breeder who sold his birds to pet stores, and this was Winston's fate.

Within a few weeks after being hatched, he was separated from his doting parents and placed in another nearby aviary, which also contained several other weaned birds. While there, he was spoon-fed by the breeder's wife until he could feed himself. This period of hand raising also helps these aggressive little parrots to become accustomed to being handled.

Then one day the breeder's wife entered the aviary as usual, then she picked Winston up and shoved him into an aerated carton, which was promptly sealed. Of course, we can only surmise how he must have felt. But worst was yet to come. The carton that contained him was then placed in a courier van, and after almost four hours of lurching around in almost total darkness, his destination was reached.

It was a pet store in Port Augusta, a large town that straddles the far upper reaches of the Spencer Gulf in South Australia. It has a population of around fifteen thousand, and as its name implies, it was a seaport. But in a short space of time, the ships grew too large to safely navigate the shallow, narrow gulf water. Nowadays, the town's unique location is its largest asset, because almost everything travelling, either by road or rail, to and from east to west or from south to north of this great country must invariably pass through it.

As soon as the courier van stopped there, Winston was whisked straight into the pet store where the carton containing him was opened. While temporarily blinded by the glaring light, someone picked him up and chucked him into a small birdcage before he could retaliate. Thankfully, the cage did contain food and water. After quenching a severe thirst, he had a look around and was puzzled by what he saw. He was familiar with the people wandering around and several of the other birds on display, but he had never seen any of the other strange creatures before.

Within a few days, he too became accustomed to the store's routine. The lights came on when its staff commenced work, and they were turned off at the day's end. The main lighting remained off from midday on Saturday until the following Monday morning or on public holidays. Although during the day, some light did filter in through the store's large front windows. But where the birds were kept, right down the back of the store, semi-darkness prevailed.

When the staff turned up for work, the store came alive as they cleaned out the cages and provided fresh food and water to their eager captives. Once this was completed, the doors were opened to the public.

Winston had been at the store for only a short time when a very unfortunate incident occurred. Up until this happened, he was the centre of attention because he was the only rainbow lorikeet there. Everyone was smitten by not only his bright colours but also his lively personality. Then a young couple and two children entered the store intending to purchase a small bird. While the couple were looking over what was on offer, one of their children, an inquisitive young boy, made the mistake of poking a finger into Winston's cage. Feeling threatened, he bit it and drew blood. Well, that child screamed with pain. While his mother frantically tried to console him, his father stood tall, puffed out his chest, and threatened in no uncertain terms to sue the store for gross negligence. After they left empty-handed, the overly anxious store manager hung a sign on the front of Winston's cage that read, 'Beware. I bite.'

After this happened, he still drew a lot of attention, but once a potential buyer noticed the sign, they would saunter off to look for something a little less intimidating.

Thus, he remained cooped up in a small cage at the store for almost a year, and during this period, his behaviour changed. He was once a lively, active little parrot, but now he had grown sullen and withdrawn.

CHAPTER TWO

That was until a dear old lady entered the store. Everyone in town who knew her, including the town mayor, called her Aunty. Before retiring, she worked for many years as a caregiver at an old-age facility at the local Aboriginal mission. She had come to the pet store intending to purchase a little puppy or kitten for companionship, because she had outlived her husband, her immediate family, except for a daughter who lived elsewhere, and a small circle of close friends. Having lived in the town all her life, she had not visited the pet store before. Among the many weird and wonderful creatures on display, they did have several cute puppies and kittens for sale. While trying to settle on which one to choose, she inadvertently wandered into the very noisy bird section and was amazed by the variety on show. There were budgerigars, canaries, finches, lovebirds, and cockatiels.

One of them especially caught her eye; it was a rainbow lorikeet, which brought back many fond memories.

The last holiday she and her husband took together, they drove to Queensland to visit their daughter. During their enjoyable stay, they also went to a private zoo, which also had a large walk-through bird aviary that contained a flock of rainbow lorikeets. It was one of those places where the visitors were encouraged to closely interact with the birds by holding up trays of their favourite food, and the visitor soon found themselves swarmed by those colourful riots of the sky. Aunty did not know what she enjoyed the most: watching the rainbow lorikeets or the gleeful expressions on the faces of those feeding them.

She returned to the puppies and kittens but still could not decide between the two. So she went back to the rainbow lorikeet. A helpful shop assistant explained the circumstances surrounding the warning sign on its cage. She also said in all her dealings with the bird, it had never even attempted to bite her. Then she went on to say they were very excitable birds, and this excitement could quickly turn to aggression if they felt threatened.

Still undecided on what to do, Aunty left the store, and while walking the short distance to her car, she suddenly decided to rescue that sad little rainbow lorikeet. Apart from buying the bird, she also purchased a large cage that sat on a stand, which had wheels attached and could be moved around with ease.

The store manager, realising she had never cared for a bird before, was most forthcoming with helpful advice, and he also gave her a fact sheet on caring for them, before advising her how the rainbow lorikeet was different than most other parrots, in that they require a special diet and more effort in their daily care. As a rainbow lorikeet owner, he went on to say, 'You will need to prepare their special food and spend considerable time cleaning its living space, because they are not only messy eaters but also have messy toilet habits.' Then he said, 'This is the main reason why some people only feed them seeds, which is not their natural food, and in my opinion, this is tantamount to animal cruelty, because they do not derive sufficient nutrition from it, which leads to shortened lives.'

As she was paying him for the bird, its special food, the cage, and some toys for the bird to play with, she asked him how long her bird might live, and he told her that most rainbow lorikeets in captivity live about ten to fifteen years. She did a quick calculation and was daunted by the fact she would have to reach at least ninety-five years old to fulfil that lifelong commitment. Then again, it would have been about the same had she purchased a puppy or kitten, she thought.

She then asked what the bird's sex was, and he said, 'It is impossible to visually tell the difference between a male or female rainbow lorikeet, but your bird is a male because its breeder does establish their sex by DNA testing before he sells them.' Upon parting, he also told her they love fruit.

Because the birdcage was far too big for her small car, they would deliver everything to her home in an hour. She left the store and walked to a nearby supermarket and purchased an assortment of fruit before returning to her car.

During the short drive home, buyer's remorse began to cloud her mind. Trying to put this aside, she concentrated instead on choosing a name for her new companion. Seeing it was a boy, several boyish names crossed her mind before she chose Winston for no other reason than it seemed appropriate.

She had been home for a short while when the delivery van arrived, and its driver, a conscientious young man, carried both sections of the birdcage indoors then assembled it, as directed by Aunty, by a window in the kitchen. An excitable Winston was already in the cage, and so were his toys. The climbing toys hung from its top while others were on its floor. She also noticed he seemed to gravitate towards toys that made a noise.

Another feature of the birdcage was, its food and water trays could be removed and replaced from outside, and there was no need to put your hands in harm's way, except when cleaning its interior. After the cage was assembled, the young man fetched a box of especially formulated rainbow lorikeet food from the van. It came in powdered form, and he explained, 'It can be given to them dry, as we do at the store, or a little water and honey can be added to it. Either way, they love it.' Upon departing, he told her, almost as an afterthought, 'They also love eating the nectar within the eucalyptus flowers, which is one of their primary sources of food in the wild.'

After giving Winston some water, his special food, and a slice of apple, she made a cup of tea and sat at the kitchen table, deep in thought, while Winston climbed about on his hanging toys.

CHAPTER THREE

Winston had been at Aunty's place for several weeks without incident. Initially, he would always feint to bite her whenever she cleaned the interior of his cage with a sponge and warm, soapy water. But this was as far as his aggression ever went, and within a few days, he stopped doing this.

Then one day, while cleaning his cage, he stepped onto her hand, then before she could move, he raced up her arm and perched on her shoulder. She froze with fear and dared not move in case he flew off. If that happened, there was no way, she thought, due to old age, she could recapture him. Then it happened! He took flight and flew around the kitchen then down the passageway before returning to settle on top of his cage. Rather than startling him by trying to pick him up, she decided to get his favourite fruit, a fig, from her own tree, which she had in the fridge, and she used that to coax him back into the cage.

From that day on, she let him out to exercise indoors almost every day. He mostly flew in and out of all the rooms, including the sleep-out, before settling somewhere. Mostly it was on top of an open door. If he could not be seen or heard, he was usually up to no good. Most parrots, both large and small, can be very destructive, and Winston was no exception. He was more than capable of reducing paper into a pile of confetti in a flash, stripping the plastic coating off power cables in a blink, trashing the pretty flowers in the vases within a few seconds, and decimating the contents of a fruit bowl in minutes. On one occasion, she heard Winston screaming in the bathroom, and she found him stuck in the toilet bowl, unable to fly or climb out. Apart from often getting up to mischief, he was also a loving little individual with a lively personality. Often when Aunty was watching daytime television, Winston would curl up in the nape of her neck and take his mid-afternoon nap.

Aunty had lived in the same house for almost sixty years. She and her husband, who was a train driver and a passionate fisherman, moved into it soon after their marriage. They were both twenty years old at the time and would soon go on to have their only child. For many years, they rented their house from the railways and purchased it when they placed all their rental cottages on the market.

It was situated on the outskirts of town. Along its front was a footpath and road, then there was a wire fence which bordered the train marshalling yards; just beyond this broad expanse of railway lines was the narrow gulf waters.

Ever since Winston almost drowned while sneaking a bath in the toilet, Aunty wheeled his cage out onto the front veranda and then put a large dish of water in it for him to bathe. She did this several days a week, and she usually left him out there for an hour or two. Having not seen motor vehicles before or people riding bikes of every kind or locomotives and trains or low-flying aircraft or boats on the nearby gulf water, he was mesmerised by their sight and sounds. Nor could he look without envy at all the different species of free birds that frequented the birdbath in the front yard.

Nearly every Sunday morning, Aunty attended church. After this, she drove to the Westside Cemetery to place flowers on her husband's grave. She had done this hundreds of times before without noticing the many flowering eucalyptus trees near the cemetery. So she broke a few branches off one to take home to Winston then hung them in his cage, and he, having not had the opportunity to even see them before, instinctively knew what they were. What was also amazing was his climbing ability as he foraged among the hanging branches. His legs and feet, with their sharp nails, along with his strong parrot beak, were all utilised as he gathered the nectar within the flowers with his unique brush tongue.

This too is another defining characteristic of the rainbow lorikeet. It is an incredible adaption that allows them to make nectar, with which bees also make honey, their primary source of food in the wild. They also use their tongue to drink, while other parrots scoop up water with their beak and raise the head to swallow. The rainbow lorikeet dips its tongue into the water so the brushlike bristles, which are called papillae, at its end can collect it, then they withdraw their tongue and swallow. This is an important feature for a bird as arboreal as they are, because it also allows them to gather dew or raindrops from tree leaves rather than spend vulnerable time exposed while drinking surface water on the ground.

CHAPTER FOUR

After being together for almost two years, Winston suddenly began screaming like a spoilt child whenever he wanted attention, and a screaming rainbow lorikeet is difficult to ignore. He screamed when he wanted to be released from his cage; he did the same when he wanted to go out on the veranda. He even screamed to get Aunty off the phone and computer or just to remind her he was also in the room.

Of course, when this unnatural behaviour first arose, Aunty made the mistake of giving in to his demands, which only served to exacerbate the problem. There must be a reason, she thought, so she approached the pet store for some advice, but they could not offer any. In desperation, she then phoned the man who bred Winston, and he told her screaming was a learned behaviour, not a natural one, and it was also the easiest behavioural problem anyone could accidently teach their bird. He suggested she look on the Internet, and she did. Of course, there were some claiming to be experts at solving rainbow lorikeet behavioural problems, such as biting, excessive feather plucking, and screaming, but their advice was confusing. While others gave advice in order to sell products that promised to solve the problem overnight.

Then as luck would have it, a neighbour who lived in a retirement home just a few doors further down the street paid her a visit. Her name was Grace; she was also a widow, who was a foster parent to many children during her life. Both Aunty and Grace went to the same church. Grace usually called around at least once a week for tea and cake. If Winston was out of his cage, he would join them too, and Grace could think of few things more entertaining than Winston. She adored him, and sometimes he would settle on her shoulder and play with her earrings.

Aunty told Grace about Winston's newly found habit of screaming for attention. Then Grace suggested she should treat him like a naughty boy and banish him to a corner whenever he screamed. She asked Aunty what normally had a calming effect on Winston. Aunty thought for a moment before telling her he always fell silent when she covered his cage with his night blanket.

'Well, that's it!' Grace exclaimed. Then she continued, 'Whenever he resorts to screaming, just cover his cage regardless of the time of day. By doing this, he will soon realise the only reward he will receive for this annoying behaviour is total darkness.'

Initially, Aunty considered this measure a little too extreme and was reluctant to implement it until Winston forced her hand. As soon as he started screaming, she covered his cage, and he stopped immediately. If he did it while out of his cage, she picked him up then put him back in the cage and covered it. He would remain covered for a half hour or so. After a week of this tough love, Winston soon realised screaming would not gain him the attention he craved.

Like most pet owners, Aunty spoke to Winston as if he were a person, and over time, he began to imitate her by saying simple things like 'Good morning, Winston' or 'Pretty boy Winston' and 'Naughty boy Winston'.

While buying his special food at the pet store, she told the manager Winston could talk, and he said, 'Some rainbow lorikeets can talk, while others may never say a word, so consider it a bonus.'

Even though Winston required more effort in his daily care than most other parrots, Aunty felt this was a small price to pay for his companionship. While most other parrots only require seed, fresh water, and their living space only cleaned occasionally, the rainbow lorikeet requires a special food that must be prepared daily along with some fruit. While eating fruit, they bite a chunk out of it, then they crush it within their strong beak to extract the juice, which they swallow before discarding the fruit pulp with a flick of the head, and it flies in every direction. Because their diet is so moist and their digestive tract is short, what goes in one end is quickly squirted out the other. This trait, along with their messy eating habits, means considerable time is spent cleaning in and around their cage to keep them healthy and happy.

Aunty ensured Winston received the best of care, because she soon found he was a unique individual with a playful personality, and she encouraged these aspects rather than having him continually cooped up in a cage as a live ornament.

CHAPTER FIVE

Quite late one night, the lights suddenly came on, and shortly after, Winston heard strange voices. He could not see what was going on because the cage was covered with its night blanket, although some light did filter through its folds. Then the lights went off again. He heard doors close, then a motor vehicle leaving the driveway, and then silence.

Unbeknownst to Winston, Aunty suffered a stroke while in bed, which paralysed her right arm and leg. So she phoned for an ambulance before phoning Grace to ask if she could look after Winston while she was in hospital, which was something she had done for two days once before.

Being an early riser, Aunty normally removed the night covers from his cage shortly after sunrise. But today this did not occur until almost midday, and Grace uncovered him instead, which Winston found rather confusing. After replenishing his food and water, she left. Just before sunset, she returned and did the same before covering him. The fear of him not returning to the cage prevented her from freeing him to fly around indoors for a short while. Within three days, Winston resorted to screaming again, and Grace put a stop to it by the usual means. On the fourth day, Grace replaced the soiled newspaper on the floor around his cage before attempting to clean its interior, but Winston became excessively territorial, and his aggressive body language indicated a bite was imminent.

While all this was going on, and because the local hospital did not have a stroke unit, the Royal Flying Doctor Service flew Aunty to an Adelaide hospital that did, where they ascertained the stroke was not life-threatening, but it will leave her with the inability to walk or move the right arm. So it was decided, and very much against her wishes, to transfer Aunty from the hospital to a high-dependency care facility nearby.

Grace had been looking after Winston for almost a fortnight. Then one morning, she arrived accompanied by a middle-aged woman, who Winston had seen once before. It was Aunty's daughter, who had driven down from Queensland with her husband to put her mother's affairs in order.

On the following morning, Grace wheeled Winston's cage out to the veranda. A short time later, the daughter, along with her husband, arrived in a car, towing a large trailer. Then all morning, they carried items from the house and loaded them onto it. About midday, another man arrived, and he spent considerable time in the house before they all left.

During the following morning, a large truck backed up the driveway, then two workmen alighted from it. For the next few hours, they carted everything out of the house, including its window coverings, and loaded it all into the removal truck. When finished there, they then cleaned out the shed and left.

That evening, Grace, and not without much sadness, wheeled Winston's cage back into the empty house, knowing this would be the last time she would see her little friend, because Aunty's daughter had decided to take him back to Queensland. She only decided this after she realised Grace could not take him because she lived at a retirement home that disallowed pets.

Quite early the next morning, the daughter came into the kitchen and removed Winston's night cover from his cage. Then instead of transferring him into a much smaller cage for transportation as promised, she wheeled his cage out into the backyard, where she opened one of its smaller auxiliary doors, instead of the much larger main door. Then she strode off without looking back.

At no stage did she intend to take Winston back to Queensland; she only said this to dispel her mother's concern for his welfare. In fact, she, whether through ignorance or indifference, thought she, without considering the dire consequences, was doing Winston a favour by setting him free. But he had never previously fended for himself. Not only did he now have to find his own food and water, he also had to avoid the skulking cats and lurking birds of prey, because the rainbow lorikeet usually approaches life fearlessly, which is not always to their benefit. The other thing that would affect him was the harsh local environment after having spent most of his life sheltered indoors. Nor had he ever flown outdoors, and this, coupled with his lack of physical fitness, could also prove detrimental to his survival.

CHAPTER SIX

After the daughter opened the cage door, Winston just stood there and looked around the unfamiliar backyard. In one corner was a shed; in the other was a huge fig tree, which still bore fruit, although much had already dropped to the ground, plus there was a birdbath and several potted shrubs. He could also see Aunty's car and her husband's boat and trailer in the driveway. The person who purchased the furniture had also bought these.

Despite being envious of the freedom enjoyed by all the different birds that frequented the birdbath in the front yard, he now was faced with the same opportunity but found himself undecided on what to do next. He compromised by flying to the fig tree and feasted on its sweet fruit until he could eat no more. It was a warm day, so he perched high up within the coolness of the tree canopy. While there, some men took the car and boat away.

He stayed up in the fig tree all day. From this high vantage point, he could see into several neighbouring backyards. Some of them had dogs and cats lazing about. Looking to the southeast, he could see the Flinders Ranges that were thrust up from the plains by tectonic plate movement during ancient times.

When looking out over Aunty's house roof, he could see the large railway marshalling yards, and today they were particularly busy, because several times annually, hundreds of military troops converge on the town to carry out war manoeuvres on the huge army base situated about ten kilometres from town. The troops come by road, and their heavy equipment, such as battle tanks, armoured troop carriers, field guns, and earth moving machinery come by rail. It is offloaded at these train marshalling yards and then transported out to the army base on heavy haulage trucks. When the war games are completed, usually within four to six weeks, this procedure is repeated in reverse. Either way, this unloading and reloading normally take a few days. Some of this equipment are even railed down from Darwin.

Winston's fascination for all this activity never waned as he watched them drive most of the equipment off the flat-top railway wagons onto road transporters, while others were lifted off by a large crane.

Just beyond the marshalling yards was the gulf waters. Looking north, he could see high red soil cliffs on one side of the gulf; on the opposite side were mangroves and tidal flats. Beyond these was the sparsely vegetated sandhill country. A little further on from this was a single-track railway bridge that traversed the narrow gulf waters. Casting his eyes further south, there was the road bridge that enjoined the east side of town to the west side. Adjacent to this, several pleasure boats were moored where once ships from many parts of the world took on or disgorged their precious cargoes.

During the early afternoon, he did what most birds do, whether they were in the wild or in captivity, and that was having a nap. As he slept, a northerly wind sprung up, which awoke him, and feeling thirsty, he flew down to the backyard birdbath for a drink before returning to the comparative safety of the fig tree. Having never flown in the outdoors before, he was surprised by the difficulty to maintain a straight line of flight in windy conditions. Just before sunset, he returned to his cage to sleep but found this almost impossible to do without being covered with his night blanket as it was a moonlight night.

Eventually, he fell asleep then was awakened by a strange tinkling sound, and then something began to violently shake his cage. Luckily, Aunty's daughter failed to open the large front door of the cage and instead opened a much smaller auxiliary door. Then a big ginger cat wearing a collar with a dainty little bell attached to it sprung up onto the front of the cage then desperately tried to force its large head through the narrow auxiliary door opening. Winston's escape was blocked off. Even if he could, he ran the risk of flying blindly into an obstacle because the night vision of a rainbow lorikeet is no better than ours.

Instead of cowering in anticipation of his probable fate, he did something the cat never expected. Winston decided offence was the best defence; he launched himself onto the cat's face and clung onto it with his sharp nails while biting its nose several times with all his might. Well, that cat gave out a blood-curdling cry and dropped to the ground before skulking off into the night. Now beset with hypervigilance, Winston did not sleep during the remainder of that night.

After this terrifying encounter, he abandoned his cage. Even so, he did not venture too far from Aunty's house for three reasons. Firstly, there was the fig tree, the only readily available source of food he was aware of; secondly, he was not yet strong enough to fly long distances, especially in windy conditions; and thirdly, he felt exposed and vulnerable, because the rainbow lorikeet is intrinsically a flock bird and thus seeks safety in numbers. He found a safe place to sleep. It was inside a pipe cross arm of a power pole only a short distance from Aunty's house.

CHAPTER SEVEN

During the following two weeks, he not only extended his time on the wing but, more importantly, also the ability to fly safely in windy conditions. By now, the days were becoming shorter and the nights cooler. The fig tree began dropping its overripe fruit and shed its leaves. Winter was fast approaching. He must find another food source because the fallen figs were rotting and covered with nasty ants. It was at this point he decided to venture further afield.

Port Augusta was acclaimed in the past for its swarms of flies and blinding dust storms. Back then, the township itself had very few trees. Most had been cut down to satisfy the growing demand for building timber, fence posts, and firewood. But all this changed for the better about four decades ago when a huge tree planting programme was enthusiastically implemented. Today the township is a verdant oasis surrounded by dappled native vegetation, saltbush plains, tidal flats, salt pans, and vivid red sand dunes. Apart from planting hundreds of eucalyptus trees, they also planted myall trees, red flowering bottle brushes, and various types of acacias. All these trees and bushes have now matured, providing food, shelter, plus nesting sites for many different species of birds, including waterbirds. All this takes place on the mangrove-fringed shores of the far upper reaches of the Spencer Gulf in South Australia and within sight of the beautiful Flinders Ranges that are no further, as the crow flies, than twenty kilometres away.

Winston was close to Aunty's house, which was situated about two kilometres from the town's central business district, and he intended to go there in search of food. When flying, the rainbow lorikeet has only one speed, and that is flat out, because they are vulnerable to bird of prey strikes when on the wing. In this fashion, he flew from tree to tree until he arrived in town.

Apart from its imposing edifices and human activity, along with their motor vehicles, the other thing that surprised him was the vast array of bird species that also lived within the town. Of course, he had seen many of them before, while others were a complete mystery, especially the waterbirds that congregated around the town's foreshore.

Near there, he also saw a tree that had flowers which looked like the ones Aunty occasionally brought home to him. He flew over to it, and no sooner had he landed, several birds, almost twice his size, vigorously set upon him. They were red wattlebirds that also eat nectar and pollen within the flowers with their long pointy tongue. They are a noisy, domineering bird that vigorously chases other bird species away from their flowering and nesting trees within their perceived territory. Winston left in a hurry and found another flowering tree a little further on.

While climbing about, foraging, he heard a familiar sound. It was the unmistakable sound of rainbow lorikeets in the adjoining tree. He became very excitable and quickly joined them but soon found out it was a mistake.

The rainbow lorikeet was not a native to this region due to its hot arid environment. But several years ago, five of them accidently escaped from a local bird fancier's backyard aviary, and they had multiplied into a flock of about twenty birds that had thrived among the town's irrigated trees.

Winston assumed he would be accepted by them without considering the hierarchical complexity within a tight-knit flock of rainbow lorikeets, where the dominant males rule the roost. They were the ones that attracted the females for breeding, and if they felt their position was threatened by another vagrant male, they would react in the only way they know how. Three dominant males set upon Winston at once and forced him out of the tree onto the ground where they continued to attack. Luckily for him, a stray dog attracted by the melee came by, and his attackers flew off. Now barely able to fly, Winston slowly headed back to his power pole near Aunty's place. There was no doubt had the dog not intervened, Winston might have been killed.

This violent behaviour is not uncommon. In their natural habitat, those rainbow lorikeets that pair up for breeding settle in trees with hollows in which they nest, while the bachelors and spinsters roost in separate trees. Many of these never pair up for any number of reasons, but if they encroach upon the nesting trees, they too are harshly dealt with, as are other bird species. Those lizards, which are not only proficient tree climbers but also consummate nest robbers, also receive the same treatment regardless of their size. The common goanna is an opportunist that not only steals eggs but also takes small hatchlings from the nest if their parents are absent.

It took Winston several days to recover from the encounter with the local rainbow lorikeets. So instead of going back into town, he searched in the opposite direction and discovered only a short distance away another clump of eucalyptus trees laden with flowers. They were also swarming with native honeybees, ants, and other nectar-eating birds, such as the singing honeyeaters.

These flowering trees are very clever. They do not only produce beautifully delicate flowers, which contain the pollen-bearing organ consisting of the filament and anther, which is called the stamens, but in order to convey the pollen, which are fine grains of yellowish powder or spores, from flower to flower, they also produce sweet nectar, which entices all honey-eating species, including ants, to unconsciously carry out this cross-fertilisation for them.

This clump of trees sustained Winston for about three weeks or until their flowers became dry, and by this time, winter had set in. He had yet to experience the local adverse climatic conditions because he had spent most of his life in the pet store or at Aunty's house, and both had reverse cycle air-conditioning.

It can get very cold in Port Augusta, where the night temperature can often dip south of zero degrees Celsius. In contrast, the summers are long and extremely hot. Sometimes the temperature can hover around forty degrees Celsius, and for two to three weeks, it soars above that. Sometimes it almost nudges fifty degrees Celsius, and when this occurs, many birds fall from the sky. Even the hardy kangaroo has difficulty surviving these heatwaves. Now weakened by lack of food and water, they too can perish, because their only means of cooling themselves is by constantly licking saliva onto the inside of both arms. But it hardly ever rains during summer, and they become severely dehydrated, which prevents them from sufficiently wetting their arms for it to be effective.

CHAPTER EIGHT

By now, Winston had experienced freedom for almost eight weeks, but he still wanted to engage with people for the obvious reason that they had provided him with food, water, shelter, and entertainment for almost his entire life. He began to fly out of nowhere and settle on the shoulders of complete strangers as they walked along the footpath near Aunty's place. Of course, this startled them, but he continued to do it, and before long, it became common knowledge in that area of town. He even landed on the shoulders of several elderly people walking around the nearby retirement village where Grace lived. She also heard stories about the rainbow lorikeet that lands on people's shoulders, scaring the living daylights out of them, before it takes off. But she, believing Winston was in North Queensland, never gave it a second thought. Although, he was never far from her mind, because one day, while visiting Aunty, she took some photos of Winston then had one of them enlarged and framed before hanging it on the wall above her television set.

When there were no eucalyptus flowers remaining close by, he was compelled to look elsewhere. Upon noticing a small settlement—it was the local Aboriginal mission—about three kilometres further on towards the Flinders Ranges, he flew there and came across the small flock of the town's rainbow lorikeets that attacked him. Only this time, they ignored him because they too were hard-pressed to find sufficient food, as most flowering native trees were dormant during winter, the majority of flowers in spring and summer, but there was one local eucalyptus species that produced small yellow flowers during both late autumn or early winter, and there were a few of these scattered around the mission.

The main problem with these trees were the birds of prey, such as the falcons and hawks, who also knew they would attract honey-eating birds. They lay in wait, either by circling high above or from some other obscure launching site. Their first attack is usually a feint designed to flush their quarry out of the relative safety of the tree canopies into flight. It is here that their far superior speed on the wing comes into play. Usually, it is the young birds that panic while the wiser birds remain within the tree canopy and remain motionless. Through observation, Winston soon learned this too.

Birds do have incredible daylight vision. It is far superior to our own. To give you some idea of this, here's an example: when we look at a mountain about ten kilometres away on a clear day, we can vaguely see it has some sort of vegetation on its slopes, while a bird looking at it from the same vantage point can plainly see most of the different plant species growing there. That is why the birds of prey and, despite their stealth, are usually spotted well in advance. The first bird that sees it then raises the alarm by making a unique warning sound which alerts all birds in the vicinity.

The most dangerous birds of prey are the raptors, such as the aforementioned hawks and peregrine falcons. Some owls, being nocturnal, can also be deadly when least expected. There is another predator that hardly ever gets mentioned, and that is the butcherbird. They are only slightly bigger than a rainbow lorikeet, and they prey on small birds, mammals, lizards, small snakes, and large insects. It normally hangs its prey in a small tree fork or bush so it can tear it apart with its strongly hooked beak, hence their name, and yet they are beautiful songsters.

The problem with having to forage for food at the Aboriginal mission was the distance Winston had to fly each day. Moreover, he had to fly over open sand dune and salt pan country where the trees were sparse. So he looked for a similar power pole, in which he already lived, much closer to the mission and eventually found one. When entering its pipe cross arm, he found it occupied by a pair of birds that looked remarkably like his own kind. They were the hardy purple-crowned lorikeet, which is a native to this region. Unlike the rainbow lorikeet, which are normally a native of the verdant coastal regions of Australia, these short-tailed little bright-green parrots have adapted to surviving in harsh environmental conditions. They too have multicoloured feathers, although they are not as vibrant as the rainbow lorikeet. They also eat nectar, pollen, plus native fruits and berries.

Winston eventually found another vacant power pole a little further on. Although, within a week, the flowers at the mission, having served their reason for being, became dry and shrivelled. So having no other option, he returned to his old haunts, where he resumed his game of landing unsuspectedly on the shoulders of pedestrians walking near Aunty's old place.

Grace heard about this too, and she, along with another retirement village resident, walked the short distance to investigate. Sure enough, there was a rainbow lorikeet perched high up on a gently swaying power line. Then it flew down and settled on Grace's shoulder, which shocked her. What it did next shocked her even more. It immediately began to play with her earring. Now totally beside herself, she asked, 'Is that you, Winston?' She then tried another tactic and said 'Pretty boy Winston' three times. There was a lengthy pause before it stopped playing with her earring and said in his familiar hoarse voice, 'Pretty boy Winston.' Well, all Grace could say, over and again, was 'Your poor little bird' before becoming completely overwhelmed with emotion. Now totally confused by this, her companion, who was ignorant of the circumstances which led to this outburst of tears, tried to console her. In the meantime, Winston flew away.

After a while, Grace regained a semblance of composure, although her mind was filled with questions. About two weeks after Aunty's daughter returned to Queensland, Grace phoned her to check on Winston's welfare; she was told he had settled in well. Why did she tell such a barefaced lie? Or did her mother know what had happened? As she walked back to the retirement village, she noticed a For Sale sign in the front yard of Aunty's vacant house.

As soon as she arrived home, she phoned the daughter and told her that contrary to what she said, Winston was still in Port Augusta. There was a long silence before the daughter explained that Winston escaped when they tried to transfer him from his large cage into a smaller one for transportation in their car. She only lied because the truth would break her mother's heart, and it would also adversely affect her medical condition. Grace asked what she would tell her mother if she ever visited her in Queensland; she was told this was unlikely because her medical specialist said she was virtually bedridden. Grace had her suspicions but held her tongue because it might have been an accident. They both decided to keep the truth to themselves and not tell Aunty for her own benefit.

CHAPTER NINE

By now, winter had set in. On some nights, ice formed on birdbaths and surface water. After being reacquainted with Winston, Grace would often walk down to where she met him. Sometimes he was there, and he would always settle on her shoulder and play with her earrings for a little while before flying off. There were many times she did not see him for several days on end. During these periods, she worried about his welfare, then just when all hope seemed lost, he, from out of the blue, would appear again and gladden her heart. When considering his past, his ability to survive amazed Grace. If not for her painful arthritis hips, which the cold weather aggravated, especially the bone-chilling southerlies that seem to come up from the South Pole, she would have looked for Winston more often.

There were now no eucalyptus flowers anywhere, and the energy expended in searching for them could not be replaced. At this point, he took notice of what the other nectar-eating birds were eating. Most were feeding on the nectar, stamens, pollen, flower blooms, and buds, along with some unripe seeds, in the town's ornamental gardens. He also saw the mulga parrots that do not eat nectar and the purple-crowned lorikeets that do, eating the small berries or fruit on some native bushes. So despite not knowing what was safe or harmful, he tried them all without any ill effects. In fact, most of them were very palatable.

After one of these garden forays, he was returning to his power pole for the night, and there, perched upon it, was a butcherbird. Apparently, it noticed Winston's movements and now lay in wait for him. Now aware of it and the danger it posed, Winston flew on before landing on the power line some distance away. Unless on the cusp of starvation, a butcherbird will not usually attack a rainbow lorikeet because of their size. Normally, they look to prey on easier-to-handle birds. Although, sometimes their ambition exceeds their capabilities, and they attempt to take down a larger bird, usually without success, but the attempt can inflict an injury which must be avoided, as even a minor one could, due to infection, become fatal. So Winston kept his distance; they were at a stalemate with nightfall looming, and then it became too dark to fly.

Winston was stranded on a power line out in the open when he should have been sheltering from the cold within the steel pipe cross arm of his power pole. Anyhow, he had no way of knowing if the butcherbird had left the area, or was it waiting in the pipe ready to ambush him?

According to the locals, that night was the coldest in living memory. Many birds caught out in the open, without any overhead protection from the heavy frost, suffered from hypothermia. Although somehow, Winston survived albeit at a cost. Normally, after a frost in this region, the day would usually begin with clear blue skies and bright sunshine. Winston basked in its pleasant warmth until his body temperature regained some normality, and he then went foraging for a short time in a nearby garden.

Having not slept a wink all night, he returned to his power pole then crawled into its steel pipe cross arm and slept all day. When he awoke, his feet were very painful. In fact, he could hardly bare standing on them.

It was frostbite. This can occur when birds get a scare on a dark frosty night then panic and end up clinging to fence wires or utility lines and the like for hours. The most serious aspect of frostbite with birds is damage to their toes, and in severe cases, the toes may be partially or even completely lost. Although unsightly, most birds seem to get over such losses rather well. However, for a rainbow lorikeet, these losses can be devastating because they need strong, flexible feet and legs, along with sharp toenails, to keep themselves securely anchored when climbing trees.

The rainbow lorikeet has four toes on each foot—three points forward and one point back. The middle toe of the three that point forward is the longest and strongest. Over the next few days, the tips of his middle toes became very painful and then turned black before dropping off. Up until this happened, he could not clutch or cling onto anything because of the excruciating pain. So he hobbled about on the ground, foraging for food among the bushes and shrubs in the garden, which left him exposed to cat attacks. Once the toe tips were lost, the pain soon subsided, and within another week, the affected toes had completely healed. Shortly after this, he was back in the trees. Initially, his climbing ability was affected, but he soon devised other ways to compensate for his loss.

Late one afternoon, Winston was returning to his power pole when he saw Grace walking along the footpath; he flew down and spent a few minutes with her before continuing his way. Grace was so pleased to see him she did not notice his injuries. When he arrived at his power pole, he found it had been taken over by a pair of purple-crowned lorikeets while he was away. Looking for another suitable power pole in winter or spring was pointless because they would all be occupied by hollow-nesting birds. They had no choice other than nest in man-made structures because the old hollow-producing trees in this area were felled long ago.

Winston flew to a huge peppercorn tree situated on a sand dune embankment, which bordered one side of a salt pan that lay about halfway between the town's outer limits and the Aboriginal mission. This salt pan is about one kilometre long by a half kilometre wide. It is called Umeewarra Lake, and it is a site of significance in Port Augusta for many Aboriginal groups who have populated this region for at least forty thousand years before the arrival of the white men. During all that time, they managed to avoid leaving a physical imprint of their existence, apart from some rock and cave art, on this once pristine wilderness. Umeewarra Lake has no dwellings in proximity, and all modes of transport, including horses, are prohibited from entering its area. It is a lake in name only because it is bone dry for most of the year.

Winston had often flown across this salt pan on his way to and from the mission, which was about a kilometre further on. The isolated peppercorn tree in which he now found himself had protected him in the past. On several occasions, he was compelled to dash to it for concealment when aware of a bird of prey lurking in the vicinity. On one occasion, he stayed in it all night during a thunderstorm. From this location, which was about three kilometres from Aunty's house, he could venture much further out into the wilderness in search of more suitable food. During these travels, he saw for the first time some very strange creatures. Of course, he had no idea what they were, but he had seen rabbits, foxes, sheep, goats, kangaroos, emus, horses (some with people riding on their backs), and camels.

CHAPTER TEN

On the opposite side of the Umeewarra Lake is a main road that connects the township with the Aboriginal mission and places further on. On the other side of the road is a large tract of vacant land, which the town's early pioneers named Camel Flat.

This came about when some of them decided to import large numbers of camels and their handlers from overseas, because the camel was a far superior pack animal than anything else, especially in very dry and hot conditions. The horse and bullock drays were ideal for short haul journeys but were found wanting when attempting to travel long distances in the harsh Australian outback. While the camel was almost impervious to extremely hot conditions, they only needed to drink every other day and were not overly fussy about what they ate. So they were not only the perfect conveyance to explore the vast outback; they could also deliver supplies to the isolated cattle and sheep stations that were springing up everywhere.

Between 1870 and 1920, about twenty thousand camels were imported from the Middle East, India, and Afghanistan, along with up to two thousand cameleers. When the first of these arrived, Port Augusta was already a thriving port town, where sailing ships and later steamers unloaded their cargoes of building materials, haberdashery, pickled food, liquor, condiments, tea, and mail from the old country. Much of this would be loaded onto camel trains and transported to the remote settlements and homesteads. Sometimes these camel trains were over a hundred animals in length. Even today, and despite its modernisation, Port Augusta is, due to its unique location, still a staging post to elsewhere.

Within a short time, the cameleers realised they were being unfairly exploited by the same people who imported them. Many broke away to form their own collective transport business and established themselves on Camel Flat, where they built a shanty settlement and planted some shady trees (many of them are still there today). And being devout Muslims who spurned alcohol, they even constructed a makeshift mosque. One of the conditions of their importation was, they were not allowed to bring their womenfolk with them, and the local white women looked upon the cameleers with disdain because of their strange appearance and their religious beliefs. So they fraternised with the local Aboriginal women instead, and the legacy of these unions are still evident today.

But while the cameleers were diligently helping to build the roads and railways, they were also bringing about their own redundancy. With the advent of motor vehicles and trains, the large number of idle camels became a liability. So the government of the day decided to impose a tax on each camel to both raise revenue while reducing their number. This was then followed up by another government proclamation stating that those camels without having had their head tax paid would be destroyed. Many cameleers returned to their home country, while others stayed and took up other lines of work. But when the government began to destroy camels, many cameleers only kept what they could afford to pay tax on. Then in defiance, they took most of their beloved camels deep into the outback and turned them loose. Even today, the outback is now full of the descendants of these camels. In fact, Australia is the last place in the world where wild camels roam in large numbers.

It was one of those trees the cameleers planted long ago that saved Winston from certain death. It happened when he was returning to the peppercorn tree after searching for food. Usually, for safety's sake, he flew quite fast from tree to tree, but this morning he decided to take a shortcut by flying across Camel Flat, which was a broad expanse of undulating drift sand country. The only trees on it were those planted by the cameleers, and they were down at the far end near the Aboriginal mission.

Winston was flying in an east to west direction, with the sun at his back, when suddenly he noticed a shadow. Startled, he instantly swerved sharply, and the bird of prey's outstretched talons barely missed him. It was a deadly peregrine falcon and one of the fastest birds in flight in the world. Having missed with its first strike, it wheeled around to give chase, and by this time, Winston had stolen a break of a hundred metres. But the trees he desperately wanted to reach were at least two hundred metres away. The chase was on. Go, little bird, and Winston arrived at the trees just in time.

There is no doubt the peregrine falcon is king of the skies, but the rainbow lorikeet is king of the trees. And the falcon was about to receive a masterclass on this subject. Game on! Due to the falcon's wide wingspan, it was unable to fly within the tree canopy, while Winston, being much smaller, had no trouble flittering here or there at will. By now, the falcon was clearly frustrated and changed tactic by climbing after him, but this too was a failure because climbing was, even when missing the tips of the toes, Winston's speciality, while the falcon just clambered about. Its main aim was to flush him out of the tree into flight. This game continued sometime before the falcon gave up and left.

CHAPTER ELEVEN

The days were now growing longer; winter was coming to an end. Winston managed to survive it without having any prior experience of fending for himself in the wild. Nor did he have the benefit of being taught how to survive by other more seasoned rainbow lorikeets. Although, there were times when he felt an intrinsic longing to join the local flock of his own kind, but their initial reaction towards him prevented this. Sure, there were times when he nearly froze to death; at other times, hunger drove him to eat things he would not normally eat, including bugs, grubs, and ants.

For some time, Winston had considered exploring the west side of town, which meant a flight of about three to four hundred metres, depending on the tide, over open water. Then he thought this was too risky in view of the recent peregrine falcon attack. So he decided to fly across the gulf waters beneath the road bridge as this would prevent being spotted from above.

Early one morning, he flew to the bridge, and while doing so, he stopped at his old power pole for a short while to see if Grace was about, who he had not seen for several weeks. But she was not there, so he went on his way to the bridge, which was near the town centre, and then he crossed to the other side without any problems.

Just over the bridge was a busy intersection that had three roads heading in different directions. Wanting to avoid densely populated areas, he followed the road that headed in a southwest direction, and by chance, this road did lead to open country. About four kilometres along this road, another one branched off to the left; this led to the holiday shacks situated along the coastline, hence the name Shack Road. A little further on, another road branched off to the right, which led to the aerodrome, and then the main road went on to the nearby army base.

On the left side of this road were houses and several industrial buildings that ended about a kilometre from the intersection. From this point on, there was a broad expanse of tidal flats that were covered with scattered clumps of mangroves. This was about a half kilometre in breadth from the edge of the road to the main gulf waters, and it continued along the road for a kilometre. This was where the rural properties and undulating saltbush country began. A levee bank also ran along this side of the road to protect it from flooding during the occasional king tide. On the opposite side of the gulf, Winston would see the town wharf, then adjacent to this were immaculate lawns with several shade sails gently billowing in the sea breeze. Beyond them was a large car park and the town's biggest shopping complex.

On the right side of this road, dense housing continued for about one and a half kilometres from the intersection before they ended. About half the houses along here were built high up on an embankment. Just before them, and situated a little further back on a steep hill, was the most prominent skyline feature in town. It was a large round water tank with an ornate dome-like roof, and it sat atop a metal iron structure that rose to a height of at least thirty metres from the ground. It was erected well over a century ago to supply water to this side of town. Nowadays it is pipelined from Morgan, on the Murray River, some two hundred and eighty-six kilometres away. A distance that is stipulated on the pipeline itself only a few metres past this old water tower. When it became obsolete, they eventually turned it into a lookout tower by installing a stairway that led up to the bottom of the tank, in which they cut a large manhole, added some handrails, and then cut several viewing windows out of the tank. It served this purpose for many decades before it was deemed unsafe, so they covered the access manhole and its viewing windows with steel mesh.

Because of its prominence, this water tank cum lookout tower caught everyone's eye, and Winston was no exception. He flew up to it to investigate and found some small birds roosting inside the tank. Knowing they were harmless, he too entered the tank by squeezing through the mesh covering a viewing window and realised this was the safest place to rest or sleep on this side of town. He stayed there for a time before sallying forth in search of food. He did not have to venture far because the lookout tower had immaculately kept lawns and extensive flower gardens around its base. There were also several old date palms nearby and a large stand of eucalyptus trees. Of course, these were flowerless and would remain so for at least another two months.

Although Winston, having spent most of his life in captivity, was not aware of this, but the rainbow lorikeets that have survived for many generations in the natural world instinctively know precisely where and when the different species of eucalyptus trees produce nectar-bearing flowers. This nectar is not only one of their primary sources of nourishment; it also has a medicinal value that is just as important for the physical well-being of these high-energy birds. In fact, the bees make their honey from this same nectar, and honey or its derivatives are still used today in modern medicine, due to its antiseptic properties, to treat some infections in people.

For the next few days, Winston had no reason to go far from the lookout tower. Then early one morning, he flew back to the main road intersection, and there, behind a shopping precinct, he found an open box containing an assortment of fruit. Sure, most of it were overripe and some were spoiled, but he could not believe his luck, considering he had not eaten any fruit for many weeks. He returned to the same place the following morning and found nothing, nor was anything there the next day, but there was some on the day after that. For three days after this, there was nothing, then on the fourth day, he arrived only to find a person loading the boxes of fruits and vegetables onto a utility. This did not deter him though, and he continued to visit that place every morning where mostly there was nothing, which meant he had to glean whatever he could from the garden shrubs, bushes, and ornamental flowers around the lookout tower.

By this time, Winston had stopped landing on the shoulders of strangers after a startled old gentleman took offence and slapped him with a newspaper.

CHAPTER TWELVE

For the next few weeks, Winston did not stray far from the lookout tower. By this time, winter was making way for spring. Some of the eucalyptus trees were also aware of this seasonal change by producing flower buds that would in time bloom. These flower buds now became predominant in his diet. Their appearance also prompted him to resume the vain search for flowering trees.

He decided to follow the main road that led to the army base. At the end of the tidal flat on his left, he noticed a dirt road that ran parallel with the sealed main road, and they were separated by the aforementioned pipeline that carried on to Whyalla about seventy-five kilometres away. So he crossed the road and followed this because the homes along there were sparse. This dirt road led to the Shack Road about three kilometres further on, and halfway along, Winston came across a property like no other.

Unbeknownst to him, it belonged to a retired merchant seaman who had lived there for over forty years. During that time, he had a small cottage built on the vacant five-hectare allotment. Then he surrounded the front half with a corrugated iron fence with a gateway adjacent to the dirt road. He cleared away all the saltbush within this compound and in its place planted hundreds of native trees and bushes, which thrived in this arid environment, such as myall trees (which were his favourite), eucalyptus trees, bottle brushes, acacias, eremophilas, and old man emu bushes. In early spring, all this blossomed into a panorama of different colours, and the atmosphere filled with the sweet fragrance of acacia flowers. The remainder of this compound was covered with compacted pure white limestone crusher dust.

All the debris that fell from the plants were neatly raked into a pile around their base, where it helped to retain moisture and would eventually become mulch. It also provided habitat for insects, caterpillars, and other invertebrates, which attracted numerous species of birds that ate them, such as the white-browed babblers, yellow-throated miners, white-winged fairy wrens, magpies, white-winged trillers, and magpie larks, just to name a few.

This compound also had several large birdbaths, and adjacent to these were other stands that held trays of specially designed powdered food for nectar-eating birds. This was what really grabbed Winston's attention.

The back half of the allotment was not cleared and remained natural saltbush country, although he did put a typical wire fence around it and placed a farm gate at one end. He also planted many myall trees and acacia bushes along this fencing. During the hot months, the kangaroos and emus would come to the town's outskirts in search of water, so he installed a water trough out the back paddock, as he called it, and left its farm gate open for them. He also bought them a bale of lucerne hay every week, and it was not uncommon to see twenty or thirty roos there shortly after sundown.

The seafarer bought this property when thirty years old, and he was an able seaman at the time. Due to the combination of experience and completing all the necessary maritime courses by correspondence, he attained the shipmaster or captain's certificate when thirty-five years old. He had to wait for another two years before he was placed in command of a ship; it was a median-sized bulk grain carrier, and he was then the youngest to achieve this position within the Danish shipping company he worked for.

He never married, nor did he ever have the inclination to do so. The sea became his tempestuous mistress, and it provided everything he needed. After becoming a captain, he would sign on a ship for about three months; his employer flew him to his ship regardless of what port it was in. After completing his assignment, they flew him home again, where he would stay for around three months before being assigned to another ship. Whenever he was at sea, he wished to be home, and within a week or two of being home, he longed for the sea. So in this context, their affair was a love-hate relationship. He kept this up for almost forty years before retiring at age sixty-seven.

His cottage was situated close to the corrugated iron fence at the back of the compound. Then one day Winston went behind the cottage and found several rainbow lorikeets in a large aviary under the veranda. Alongside this was a writing desk, at which sat an old man who had a shock of snow-white hair on his head and face. On the other side were two small parrots in another cage, and two old dogs dozed near the old man's feet. They, along with the rainbow lorikeets and the two cockatiels, belonged to his widowed elderly sister who became so ill she was unable to care for them.

Winston spent all day at the captain's place and was astounded by the diverse array of birds that lived there or frequented the property, where, apart from a brief period during the afternoon, the air was filled with their songs and chatter. While there, Winston visited the rainbow lorikeets, and being very excitable birds, they conducted a screeching match with him while he clung to the wire outside their aviary, which amused the captain.

From this day onwards, he went to the captain's place every day without incident. Then late one afternoon, while he was returning to the lookout tower for the night, a hawk began to tail him. He was approaching the tidal flats at the time and was unsure whether he had the flight speed to outrun it to the lookout tower, which was still some distance away. He had seen them striking birds in flight before, and they usually took them straight to the ground. So Winston decided to take the likelihood of this happening out of play. A high tide was in at the time, and instead of flying over open ground, he flew to a clump of mangroves in the middle of the flooded tidal flats, where he took refuge and remained motionless, as if frozen, until the hawk left the area.

CHAPTER THIRTEEN

The captain's daily routine was conducted as though he was still on a ship. He rose with the sun and went to bed at sunset every day. Soon after rising, he went to the desk under the back veranda where he had coffee, and having frowned upon smoking indoors all his life, he lit up his pipe. After this, he had a light breakfast. Usually, it was two slices of toast with another coffee. Lunch was nothing special either; it was mostly a sandwich or some fruit. The evening meal was usually a home-delivered vegetarian takeaway, or failing that, it was scrambled or poached eggs on toast.

After breakfast, he fed the rainbow lorikeets and the pair of cockatiels. They ate seed, and he threw their leftover seed from the day before out to the eagerly waiting crested or topknot pigeons. With that finished, he fed his five hens and an old rooster before filling the birdbaths and replenishing the powdered nectar trays. When this was completed, he set about raking up any tree leaves and bark that had fallen during the night. He found if he did this every morning for an hour or so, he would keep abreast of this problem. Besides this, he thought it also helped to keep him fit and healthy in view of his advanced age.

Upon completing his chores, he showered and then had lunch before spending a few hours at his desk, where he either wrote environmental articles for publication or read historical novels. Other than his own language, he spoke fluently two other languages, French and German. Therefore, many on the books he read were in those languages.

At around 3 p.m., he threw grain out for the seed-eating birds before collecting the eggs at the fowl house, and then he fed the two old dogs. At 4 p.m. precisely each day, he fetched a bottle of Irish whiskey, along with some ice from inside, and after two or three measures of that, he had his evening meal before going to bed. He did not watch television, although he did have a computer, but no mobile phone.

He was a small man who stood less than average height and lithe in statue. His hair, along with his moustache and beard, had become snow white. Although, the latter two, through constant puffing on a pipe, had left tobacco stains around his mouth. He only ever left the property to get supplies. Even though he was always, and regardless of their station in life, polite to everybody, many found his general demeanour a little too severe. But after living in Port Augusta for forty years, nobody there—apart from his bank manager, his accountant, and perhaps his doctor—could honestly say they knew him.

The captain spent his childhood in Port Adelaide, where his father was a shipping agent, and their home was close to the waterfront. His fascination for ships began at an early age. Sometimes his father took him to a ship he was an agent for, and its crew often gave him a tour of their vessel. In fact, this fascination was the main reason why he left high school during his first year there. Their home was only a short walk from the docks, and instead of attending school, he frequently spent the day looking over the ships in port.

Then one day his parents were summoned to the school for a teacher-parent meeting. His father did not go as he was far too busy, but his mother did. After being ushered into an office, the headmaster joined them. After exchanging greetings, he came straight to the point and told his mother, while her fourteen-year-old son squirmed in his seat, about him frequently wagging school. All his mother could say was, she packed his lunch and sent him off to school. Then the headmaster told her, 'That may be so, but he rarely eats that lunch in these school grounds.' He went on to say her son was absent for twenty-one days during the past two months and he had been creative with the excuses for his non-attendance. According to him, he went to at least ten funerals this past term. He then acknowledged, 'There were probably legitimate reasons for some of this absenteeism, but whenever we ask for a verification note from his parents, we are told his mother could not read or write English and his father was at sea.'

Despite her embarrassment, she informed the headmaster that she was French but read and wrote English just as well as her own language. As for his father, his parents were German, but he was born here, he was a shipping agent who never went to sea. He also suggested she should consider either sending him to a boarding school, where they could keep a tight rein on him, or let him leave school.

Within a few weeks, he had his fifteenth birthday, and shortly after that, his father secured him a trainee position on a coastal freighter that transported scrap metal. Initially, he thought his prayers were answered, until the ship's captain said he was too young and not yet strong enough to take his place among the crew. In the meantime, he was to assist the ship's cook in the galley where he prepared the vegetables, set and cleared away two dining tables (one for the officer and the other for the crew), washed then wiped the dishes, washed the officer's clothes, and made their beds. He did this for a year before becoming a crew member.

He stayed with that ship for almost seven years and became a boatswain. Wanting to further his career and see the world at the same time, he applied for a position with a Danish shipping company that owned a fleet of bulk grain carriers. He then remained with that company for thirty-three years.

Earlier in his career, he returned home between voyages and stayed with his parents in Port Adelaide. They also owned a holiday shack on Shack Road in Port Augusta, and he often drove up from Port Adelaide to stay there. On one of these visits, he noticed large vacant allotments for sale, and they were going cheaply, so he bought one. It mattered not where he lived in the world because the shipping company took care of all his travelling expenses.

Then one afternoon, he was sitting at the desk under the back veranda when Winston unexpectedly landed on his computer that was also on the desk, which certainly surprised him. Of course, he had seen him many times before. Sometimes he even came close, especially if he was visiting his own rainbow lorikeets, but never this close, and the colourful little parrot did not seem intimidated by his close presence either, which convinced the captain it was probably someone's pet that had escaped. The captain also knew the first thing you must teach a pet bird was to step up onto a presented finger. So he reached over and presented an index finger, and Winston stepped promptly onto it, which confirmed the captain's suspicion. He then brought Winston closer and began speaking to him, while Winston just stared into the captain's pale blue eyes that had witnessed the best and worst in both man and nature.

Despite not knowing what sex Winston was, the captain called him little fella anyway. He spoke to Winston for quite some time. Of course, he had no idea what he was saying. But the captain told him it would be a crime to put him back in captivity as he was doing very well on his own. It was then 4 p.m., and the captain got up and went inside to get his whiskey. Winston flew back to the lookout tower for the night.

CHAPTER FOURTEEN

From that day on, whenever Winston went to the captain's place, which was almost every day, he would seek him out and land on his shoulder. Sometimes he was raking the yard or filling the birdbaths, but mostly he was sitting at his desk, either reading or writing, while smoking his pipe.

He began writing articles about environmental issues soon after retiring from the sea, and most were an account of what he saw during his many sea voyages—things like oil spills on the oceans, countries that dump their industrial and household refuse into the sea instead of committing it to land fill, or seeing a pristine, uninhabited, heavily wooded island laid bare within a year.

Initially, he wrote these articles in longhand before typing them out on the computer and sent them off to a maritime magazine, where they often appear. One of his most popular stories was about an incident that occurred on his property. He went out to the back paddock to clean the aforementioned water trough he had installed there for the kangaroos and emus when he stumbled upon a dead kangaroo. It was a mature buck that appeared very hollowed out despite there being plenty of lush wintergreen grass about. On closer examination, he noticed the big red had a large lump, about the size of a tennis ball, under its right arm. He buried the roo where it died without giving it a second thought. That was until he discovered another dead roo there about a month later. Likewise, it too had a very pronounced lump under its chin. Being a ship's captain, he was trained to deal with most medical issues that might arise at sea, so he fetched his set of surgical instruments from the house and carefully removed the lump. He put it in an airtight plastic container then took it to a local veterinarian and paid to have it sent to a pathology clinic for analysis.

Within a fortnight, he received their analytical report. In layman's terms, it stated it was an aggressive cancer that was also common in humans, which then begged the question, How could a kangaroo develop a cancer that was also prevalent in humans? Because they only eat grass or some bushes and drink surface rainwater when available. That is all; they do not eat processed food, nor are they hooked on nicotine, alcohol, or sugar. This conundrum gave him no peace until he eventually formed an opinion.

For about seventy-four years, Port Augusta had one of the largest coal-fired power stations in South Australia, which burnt millions of tonnes of low-grade brown coal during that period. While doing so, it also discharged into the atmosphere, through its smokestacks, millions of tonnes of noxious pollutants. But what goes up must come down, and when it did, it settled on roofs, where it entered the rainwater tanks. It also settled on the rivers, lakes, oceans, and farming or grazing land, where it would eventually enter the food chain. The captain was convinced of this, and he believed this was as injurious to the health and physical well-being of all life forms as global warming, yet little scientific research had been conducted on this subject.

Just before spring, many of the native trees, bushes, and shrubs would begin to bloom with different coloured flowers; some were pink, while others were white or yellow. Once this happened, the captain stopped providing man-made nectar for the honeyeaters, and he would resume this when the flowering season ended.

This took away Winston's main reason to visit his place because the eucalyptus trees near the lookout tower were also in bloom. Nevertheless, he still visited the captain and his rainbow lorikeets every other day. On one of these occasions, he found the captain placing a bowl of water and grain at the base of a tree. It was for a pair of old little corellas. They were with a large noisy migrating flock that flew over several days ago, and these were incapable of going any further. Contrary to their name, they are a median-sized white cockatoo that pair up for life, and this pair would have produced countless offspring during their long life together. But they could no longer fly well enough to fend for themselves. This was the reason he was putting food and water at the base of the tree they were in, even though he disliked them and the galah because of their destructive nature. He cringed whenever he could hear a large flock of them approaching, especially if his myall trees and acacias were in seed. Because within an hour of stripping seed pods from them, they would leave a mess that took days to rake up instead of an hour or two. Even though these little corellas and galahs were an enemy, he still extended a helping hand. Soon after putting the water and grain there, those two old birds clambered down from on high, ate and drank their fill, then climbed back up the tree again to roost.

The flower season, or spring, also herald the birds' breeding season, and for many years, the captain had fed the magpies and magpie larks, or peewees, calcium powder–laced mincemeat. They landed on the roof of a garden shed, and the magpies grabbed his attention by warbling, while the magpie larks, which were also black and white in colour, called out a loud peewee sound, hence their nickname, often with both wings lifted. When in pairs, they usually sing anti-phonetically: the male sings the first part of the song and the female sings the second. As soon as the mincemeat landed on the roof, they ate a little before loading up their beaks and then taking it to their hatchlings. They even fed their young ones for a short time after they left the nest. One old male magpie the captain called Big Beak, because his curved pointy beak was much longer than all the rest, had been calling in several times a day every spring for the past six years. Then when his young ones left the nest, he brought them over and taught them the begging game.

Then one day Winston found the captain doing something in his back paddock. Of course, he did not know what he was doing, but he was setting a cat trap. He startled the captain when he landed on his shoulder. But he greeted him with a beaming smile and a one-way conversation because he had not seen Winston for several days and thought some misadventure had befallen him. 'Good to see ya, little fella,' he said before returning to his work.

The captain believed cats had no place in any environment, let alone in an arid zone in which he lived. Because every bird-breeding season, the nocturnal cats climbed up to the birds' nests on his property during the night to attack the sitting birds. If by chance they escaped them, the cat would then devour their hatchlings. To counter this menace, he set several cat traps every year.

These traps were made with light steel mesh. They were a metre long by a half metre wide and a half metre high. One end was closed off, while its other end had a gate that dropped down. When setting these traps, this gate was raised and kept in place by a pin, which had a tripwire attached that led to the closed-off end, where it dangled from a hook. The captain tied a piece of fish on this, and when the cat pulled on it, the gate would slide shut. Simple but effective. Once caught, the local council was notified, and they would take it to their stray animal shelter. He did not have the heart to destroy them because any form of animal cruelty abhorred him; this was another reason why he abstained from eating meat. He even considered fishing with hook, line, and sinker a cruel passion to have.

Since setting these traps, he had caught well over a hundred cats, and many of them were someone's pet. Of course, lizards such as the bearded dragon and goannas also rob bird nests, but they mainly go for the eggs. The captain could tolerate them because they were an integral part of the fragile and complex arid zone ecosystem.

A few days after setting the cat traps, Winston flew out to see the captain and his rainbow lorikeets, but he could not be found, although his car was stilled parked in the driveway. His faithful old dogs—they were Rottweilers— and litter sisters were not there either. So he vainly scouted around for a while before flying down the long driveway that was flanked with tall overhanging gum trees and found the captain sitting on a deck chair at the front gate, smoking his pipe, while his two dogs lay close by. As usual, he was glad to see Winston.

The army had been conducting war games at the nearby military base for the past month, and the loud report of their tank and field guns could be clearly heard in town almost every day. Now they were transporting all their heavy equipment back to the train marshalling yards on the east side, and the captain was watching this passing parade with the enthusiasm of a young boy. Winston stayed with him for an hour or so before flying back to the lookout tower, and unbeknownst to them both, this would be the last time they would see each other.

CHAPTER FIFTEEN

On the following morning, Winston decided to cross back over to the east side of town. He intended to forage in some of his favourite trees there for a while before returning to the west side and the safety of the lookout tower. Once more, he flew across beneath the bridge and headed straight to his old home. Upon arrival, he was astounded by how much it had changed. Aunty's shrubs and bushes in the front yard were no longer there; her birdbath was gone too. In their place was a lawn on which several small persons were noisily playing. The old fig tree was still out the back, but all of Aunty's plants there had been cleared away to make way for an above-ground swimming pool and decking. There was no way of knowing whether he still remembered Aunty or her friend Grace. He probably did, because birds, in order to survive in the wild, have developed an incredible memory.

In ancient times, humans did too when still hunters and gatherers, but over time, this ability has become jaded since the advent of shops and supermarkets.

Winston flew back to the front of the house and settled on the overhead power line there. He could see they were still loading the army equipment onto flat-top railway wagons in the train marshalling yards. They were doing it with a giant crane that effortlessly picked up a hulking battle tank as though it was weightless then deftly slewed it around and placed it gently onto a wagon. It was a sight to behold and poetry in motion.

No further than thirty metres away from Winston was a damaged army vehicle on a wagon; it was a service truck that had rolled on its side. A workman, who was aware of the forecast for rain, was taping a plastic sheet over a broken window in the driver's side door.

Winston watched all this activity for a while before flying off to some nearby flowering trees, which he had foraged in several months previously. While there, the sky gradually darkened, and rolling thunder could be heard in the far-off distance. Initially, this did not alarm him because he had heard it many times before and only rarely did any meaningful rainfall. So he kept foraging until the wind rapidly strengthened. Now fearing being caught in a storm, he dashed back to Aunty's old place to seek shelter in one of the pipe cross arms on some of the power poles there but found them all inhabited by nesting birds. He had no idea what they were, but they were purple-crowned lorikeets and mulga parrots, which are also natives of this region.

By now, the wind was gale force and had already downed trees throughout the town. Now desperate, Winston, while still stranded on the power line, noticed the sheet of plastic the workman placed over the broken window of the damaged army vehicle had blown off. It was only a short distance away, and he flew through its open window and settled on the steering wheel. This was a stroke of good luck as there was no safer place to see out this storm. Shortly after nightfall, the howling wind abated considerably just before torrential rain began to fall. It was so heavy it came in through the broken window, and Winston moved to the headrest on the passenger seat to keep dry.

When the storm eventually passed, Winston had no option but to stay in the truck cabin until daybreak, because the night was very dark and light rain continued to fall. He tucked his head back and finally fell asleep. Then a very strange thing happened. He was asleep for only a short while before being startled awake by movement. The railway wagon on which the damaged truck was fastened was moving, and it was rapidly gathering speed. Winston had no idea of what to do. He could not risk injury by simply bailing out of a fast-moving truck in the dead of night. Nor would he, for fear of the unknown, relish the prospect of staying in the truck until daylight, but there was nothing else he could safely do. Of course, we have no idea of what was going through his mind, but we can surmise it would be a confronting situation for even the bravest among the brave.

Unknown to Winston, the train on which he was travelling was on its way to Darwin, some 2,550 kilometres away, and it would take about fifty hours to reach its destination. The train continued throughout the night, during which time, it did stop twice at railway sidings to allow oncoming trains to pass. When back on the main line, it soon reached its optimum speed of 100 kilometres per hour.

Daybreak only brought further despair because the stony landscape was desolate with hardly a tree in sight, and overhead, many birds of prey circled on the thermal currents. By this stage, Winston would have been very hungry. Luckily, he had plenty to drink because the heavy rain in Port Augusta came through the broken window and flooded the driver's side floor. It was not overly clean, but it was drinkable.

Two locomotives pulled the train; immediately behind them was their fuel tanker. Then there were two flat-top wagons carrying damaged army vehicles. Winston was on the second. The accommodation carriage was coupled to that, and behind this, fifty flat-top wagons carrying military equipment followed.

These long-haul trains had two driver crews. While two operated the locomotives, their relief crew ate, slept, and rested in the accommodation carriage. This system is called relay working. On this train, there were three drivers and a young trainee, or fireman, a name which originated in the steam train era, when the locomotive had a designated driver and his fireman who shovelled coal into the steam boiler. The eldest member of this crew lived in two worlds. He was an Aborigine who was deeply respected by his own people due to his profound knowledge of their lore, and in the wider community, he was a senior train driver. When he first started with the railways, he was a shunter, then he became a train guard for a few years or until the railways no longer saw the need for a brake van or a guard on their trains. But instead of taking a payout, as most of them did, he accepted their offer of becoming a trainee engineman, and that was almost twenty years ago now.

It was during one of their crew changes the men noticed Winston. The two crews met close to his wagon, and while having a normal handover conversation, one of them, while looking over the damaged truck, saw Winston perched up on a headrest. 'Look, there's a bird in there!' he exclaimed while pointing.

'Where?' the others asked.

'There, up on the headrest.'

One of them asked, 'What is it.'

Another said, 'It is a parrot.'

'It's a rainbow lorikeet,' said the oldest of the four.

'Shall I climb up there and hunt it out?' asked the engineman trainee.

'No!' exclaimed the oldest. Then he continued, 'It will leave when it is ready. It has been ordered up there.' The others gave him a puzzled look. They went on to discuss the ways and wherefores of how Winston got on their train before the eldest suggested giving him something to eat. Knowing the rainbow lorikeet loved fruit, they threw a couple of juicy apples through the broken window, and they landed on the driver's seat. Now Winston had no reason to leave the safety of the truck cabin.

Whenever the crew changed shifts, about every eight hours, they always checked if Winston was still with them. Even if this occurred during the night, they would briefly check on him with a torch, and they were careful not to spook him into flight, as they were aware of his chances of surviving in the arid red heart of this country would be minimal at best.

The train passed by Alice Springs late at night, and all Winston saw of the place was bright lights. The train changed crews there; they also refuelled both locomotives from the tanker. Their little passenger was still the focal point of their interest. In a way, he had become their mascot. Nor did they ever forget him, and for years after, they never tired of telling the story about the rainbow lorikeet that hitched a ride on their train from Port Augusta to Darwin. Of course, some believed this tale with scepticism, while the true believers embellished it even further until it became the stuff of railway folklore.

The original story was true, except for one crucial detail. Winston did not get to Darwin and spent the remainder of his life in Palmerston, which is a large town about twenty-five kilometres further south.

CHAPTER SIXTEEN

The train terminated at Berrimah, which was an outer suburb of Darwin, and when it arrived there, the crew noticed Winston had already gone. They also left the train to spend their minimum twelve hours off duty in Darwin, before being recalled to relay work another train down south. Winston left their train when it approached the outskirts of Palmerston, where it had to slow to a crawl due to a speed restriction on this section of the railway track. When this happened, Winston noticed a flock of rainbow lorikeets foraging in some fruit trees adjacent to the railway line, and he joined them.

At first, he was unnoticed, but this soon changed. He had to fight the bully boys to establish his place within the pecking order of the flock, and he soon developed a strategy to deal with them. If the body language of an aggressive male even remotely indicated an attack was imminent, he attacked first and was prepared to fight to the death. His ability to fight and win also impressed the females in the flock, because they wanted this trait to be instilled in their offspring.

Winston initially found it difficult to acclimatise to the oppressive tropical weather in the top end. It was so unlike what he had grown accustomed to. Many of the flowering native trees there were also different. Tropical fruit played a more pronounced role in the local rainbow lorikeets' diet, and it was plentiful. It grew in people's backyards and on nearby plantations. When the fruit began to ripen, the fruit bats and the rainbow lorikeets would try to be the first to plunder it. Being nocturnal, the fruit bats carried out their raids during the night and then spent the daylight hours hanging upside down usually asleep in trees.

Of course, the cats, both domestic and feral, along with the birds of prey, were no less dangerous than those down south. Winston had several close encounters with them both soon after arriving in the top end.

When studying the rainbow lorikeets' survival skills in their natural habitat, they are truly remarkable.

They intrinsically know what is healthy to eat, what is harmful, and what plants produce natural medications. All this knowledge has been handed down from one generation to the next for many thousands of years, and all this information is stored in a brain that is only slightly larger than a pea. On top of this, they must also have the instinctive ability to recognise and avoid all threats to their physical well-being, including misadventure, because they do not have the luxury of having a place to go that will reset their broken bones or close their open wounds or give them pain relief and antibiotics.

Apart from these dangers, man himself is their greatest threat. During the past 250 years, they have created global warming, and they have also dumped billions of tonnes of noxious airborne fossil fuel waste onto lakes, rivers, oceans, and land during this same period. While all this was happening, they also ruined much of the once pristine Australian bush by excessive land clearing and overstocking to the point where many natural grasses that were here 250 years ago are now extinct. Because of this, the biodiversity in the bush has been adversely affected in many regions and is irretrievable unless it is revegetated to restore the diversity it once had.

Winston had also experienced this contempt for the natural world several times. Admittedly, none were on the grand scale mentioned above. Nevertheless, they did occur, and they left a lasting impression. On one occasion, he, along with his flock mates, were not only raiding fruit trees from a backyard tree; they were also jousting with each other and making sounds only an excitable flock of rainbow lorikeets make when the owner of the fruit tree began shooting them with an air rifle. Before the flock realised what was happening, some of them had already been hit. Just as Winston took flight with the others, an air rifle slug knocked a primary feather out of his wing. It was a close call, but several of his flock mates were not as lucky. Apparently, the shooter believed his apricots were more precious than living treasures. The irony of this deadly episode was, the tree had already dropped much of its overripe fruit to the ground, and all that was required to protect the remainder was to place a net over the tree.

Winston had been in the top end for almost a year when a female flock mate caught his attention. At the time, he was perched high up resting in a tree when she settled close to him and began preening his feathers, which he reciprocated. This gentle foreplay soon kindled a desire in them both to breed. But firstly, they had to find an unoccupied tree hollow in which to make a nest, although this was not as simple as it sounded because most of the old hollow-bearing trees in and around Palmerston were felled long ago to make way for its burgeoning housing estates and commercial developments. Even so, they eventually found one in an old tree in a graveyard. The hollow was ideal because it had a small opening that would prevent the entry of any predators larger than themselves, and it would take no less than a hundred years for these hollows to form naturally in native trees.

Now that a hollow had been secured, Winston and his mate built a cosy nest in it with feathers, small twigs, pieces of string, straw, and horsehair they found at some nearby stables. They worked at a frantic pace because some local flowering eucalyptus were about to bloom and thus provide favourable conditions to raise their young.

A few days after completing the nest, his mate laid the first of two eggs, which were plain white in colour and almost spherical in form. Only the female would incubate the eggs, and she would only leave the nest for nature calls. In the meantime, Winston not only foraged for food for himself; he also fed his mate, and after about twenty-five days of incubation, he would do the same for their hatchlings as well. While his mate incubated their eggs, she continually made begging sounds when hungry or thirsty, which were close to those emitted by her young.

Their young were quite naked when hatched, but within three days, they got a covering of down, and about two weeks after this, their first feathers appeared. In the first few weeks, they grew very quickly due to their father's efforts and had an enormous appetite. Usually, when Winston entered the nest towards evening, in order to spend the night, he was so exhausted he immediately fell asleep, only to be awoken at the crack of dawn by the pleadings of his hungry brood. Sometimes when all things were quiet on the home front, he settled close to the hollow and kept watch.

If another bird, regardless of their size and species, ventured too close to their nest, both Winston and his mate would instantly become raging little furies and attack using their sharp claws and beaks as weapons. Even when an uninvited guest attempted to enter their hollow, including lizards, they rolled onto their backs to keep the offender at bay with their razor-sharp claws.

Their hatchlings opened their eyes between the tenth and fourteenth day. Now they could see their parents as well as hear or feel them entering or leaving the nest, and they begged for more food. Up until the sixteenth day, the feeding was done by Winston, then after this, his mate spent progressively longer periods away from the nest to forage.

When four weeks old, their young began to grow tail feathers, and shortly after this, wing feathers appeared, followed by head and breast feathers. At around ten weeks old, they left the nest fully feathered and able to fly. At this stage, they looked no different than their parents. Although, their parents continued to feed them for a week or two even though they were more than capable of feeding themselves. About three weeks after leaving the nest, their parents become aggressive towards them, encouraging them to join the flock to learn the required skills to survive in this hostile world.

Quite apart from growing and protecting their young, the parents must also ensure their young do not leave the nest too early. Because if not fully feathered, they are unable to fly properly, nor has their climbing skills developed. If they fell to the ground from high up, they can also incur an injury. Should this happen, the first predators on the scene are usually hordes of hungry ants. This is the reason why the parents never leave the young unattended while they are approaching full maturity.

When one parent is out foraging, the other stays behind to keep their young in check.

About two weeks after their first clutch left home, Winston's mate laid two more eggs. If conditions were favourable, they would endeavour to raise at least two clutches every breeding season while capable. Over the ensuring few years, Winston and his mate went on to raise eleven siblings and a further three were lost through hawks taking them while out of the nest. Then due to old age, they ceased breeding, and a more virile pair of rainbow lorikeets took over their nest. Although, Winston and his mate remained together until she failed to return from a foraging expedition with the flock.

When that happened, Winston was almost eleven years old, and only rarely does a rainbow lorikeet live beyond ten years in the wild, which spoke volumes about his tenacity and courage when considering all the trials and tribulations he had to contend with along the way.

Only a few weeks after his nest mate disappeared, he was with the flock foraging when, from out of the blue, a hawk swooped down. The flock scattered. Normally, these birds of prey single out the slowest flyer in the flock, and this time, it was Winston. Fortunately, the hawk was so fixated on catching Winston it took its eyes off where it was flying and flew slap bang into an overhead power line just when it was about to grab him with its lethal talons.

CHAPTER SEVENTEEN

Of course, this happened long ago, and today Winston is no longer with us. Shortly after being saved from certain death by a power line, his health rapidly declined. Perhaps the exertion of trying to outrun the hawk strained his old heart, because he suddenly experienced severe heart palpitations and breathlessness whenever he tried to fly or climb among the trees. It was so chronic he could not fly any further than about thirty metres, which not only prevented him from joining the flock on foraging expeditions but also made him easy prey. Within a few days of not eating or drinking, he began wasting away, and dehydration brought on cramps. He realised his time was up and decided to go out on his own terms. Late that same afternoon, he left the flock and headed straight to his old nesting hollow, which was about a kilometre away. When in good health, he could fly there in just a few minutes, but today it took almost an hour. He knew the breeding season had finished long ago, and he hoped the hollow was unoccupied, which it was when he eventually arrived just before sundown. He entered its narrow opening, which he had done many thousands of times in the past, then climbed down to its basement, where he made himself as comfortable as possible before going to sleep. He never awoke.

His passing should not be mourned, and instead his extraordinary life achievements should be celebrated, especially when concerning his humble beginnings. None of his achievements would not have occurred if Aunty, his original owner, had not rescued him from the pet shop. Nor would they have happened if her daughter had not set him free. Even though her motives for doing this were not honourable, in hindsight, she did him a huge favour. The alternative might have been being cooped up alone in a cage for the duration of his life. Moreover, if Aunty's daughter had opened the main door of his cage instead of the much smaller auxiliary door, a cat would have taken him on his first day of freedom. This confrontation also alerted him to the danger cats pose. Then he endured being caught out in the open during the coldest night in living memory. Although he suffered frostbite to two toes, he did survive, while many birds in similar circumstances perished.

People also contributed to his survival during his early years in Port Augusta. Aunty gave him a loving home out of pity. Her friend Grace cared for him for a short while when Aunty became incapacitated through a stroke. Then Aunty's daughter gave him freedom. Even finding the spoilt fruit behind the west side supermarket was timely because he was by then on the brink of starvation. Shortly after that, he stumbled upon the captain's place, where powdered nectar was laid on with no strings attached.

When he sought refuge from the violent storm in the truck cabin, he had no idea it was attached to a train that had a tight schedule to keep. Only a fool would have flown out of a moving train in the dead of night while rain was still falling. It was these set of unusual circumstances that trapped him on the train. When daylight came, the environment in which he now found himself appeared so inhospitable it was safer to stay with the train. Then just when starvation was about to drive him from the train, the compassion of its enginemen came to his aid.

After his arrival in Palmerston, he quickly established his place in the pecking order of the small flock he joined.

There are only two seasons in the tropical top end, the wet and the dry, and both take time to acclimatise to, especially after coming from a place with four seasons. Shortly after establishing his position and becoming acclimatised to the strange weather, he chose a breeding mate, and over the ensuring few years, they produced thirteen healthy siblings. In doing so, they had fulfilled their reason for being, or destiny, by perpetuating their species, which was something the rainbow lorikeet had successfully done for millions of years.

Even though Winston has passed away, he still lives on through his progeny in the top end. If you ever have the privilege of seeing a flock of noisy rainbow lorikeets today, in or around Palmerston, the genealogy of many can be traced directly back to Winston.

Aunty only lived for several months after experiencing her first stroke. She passed away without knowing Winston had been turned loose. Even though her friend Grace constantly visited her when she was transferred back to the local hospice unit, she did not tell Aunty the truth for fear of compromising her very frail health. The daughter also did the same for an additional reason, and that was to cover her tracks. She never intended to take Winston back to Queensland, and she only said this to calm her mother's fears for his welfare. Besides, she had no time in her busy life to care for a little parrot with an attitude and bad manners. She, along with her husband, expanded their store which sold golfing equipment with the proceeds of her mother's estate.

Grace was ninety years old when she passed away at the Port Augusta hospital. She died peacefully while surrounded by many of her foster children who were now also approaching old age. She was twice nominated for the Australian of the Year Award for her work with orphaned and abandoned children. For many weeks after Winston vanished, she kept an eye out for him without success and concluded he might have been a victim of misadventure.

After not seeing Winston at least for a month, the captain also thought he had come to grief. The captain, despite his pipe smoking and whiskey drinking, died at ninety-eight years old. He hoped to reach one hundred, but his heart had other ideas. He believed his longevity was a result of a no-meat diet, although he did eat it for the first thirty years of his life. Then his employer assigned him to a ship that was crewed by seamen from India. Apart from himself and the ship's engineer, who was Danish, the rest of the crew, including the captain, belonged to an Indian sect that religiously abstained from eating meat. For this reason alone, most of the so-called Western officers within the company were hesitant about joining this vessel. Although he had his master's ticket at the time, he was still serving as a second officer, and he volunteered for this position on this ship because he rightly thought it was a golden opportunity to advance his career.

He remained with that ship for almost four years, during which time the crew explained the benefits of eating a meat-free diet, and he had to admit, the food on that ship was excellent. They also told him many people in their communities back home live, due to their diet, beyond a hundred years. After working several three-month shifts on this ship, he no longer craved for meat. Even when back home on leave between voyages, he also abstained. He did this for the rest of his life, and the closest thing to meat he ever ate was his own fowl eggs. He believed the notion of meat being essential for a well-balanced diet was a fallacy and the opposite was probably true, when considering most meat producers nowadays, including fish farmers, used growth hormones to boost their margins.

The captain practised what he preached, and this was evident by the environment he created in which he lived. He loved the Australian bush and could see what was happening to it and its native animals and felt he had to do something. He set up a bush-based home for himself and eventually wrote articles about the degradation of the environment he had witnessed not only here in Australia but also in other parts of the world. When ninety-four years old, he wrote his last published article, and it was about the necessity to eradicate all the introduced feral foxes and cats to restore the biodiversity in the bush to its original condition.

He had no choice but to sell his beloved property after suffering his first heart attack at ninety-seven. Until his death, one year later, he resided at a high-dependency unit in Port Augusta, and true to form, he left his whole estate, which was considerable, to tree-planting projects because he believed this was another practical way to combat global warming.

CHAPTER EIGHTEEN

Winston left a lasting impression on everyone he came across along the way, such as the pet store people and the young boy whose finger he bit, then there was Aunty, Grace, the captain, even the train drivers, and also those strangers whose shoulders he unexpectedly landed on as they walked by. Confusion about where he belonged in the world was why he did this. Initially, people provided all his needs, including affection. In fact, they treated him as an equal almost, then they cast him out into a completely foreign world in which he had to find a way to survive without any prior experience. When he came upon the small flock of local rainbow lorikeets, he wrongly thought they were the answer. But his confusion deepened further when they brutally rejected him. When considering these circumstances, it is remarkable he survived at all after being released in

Port Augusta. But he did through trial and error, and this certainly impressed the captain, who had more to do with Winston after his release than anyone else in town. Sure, he called on Grace several times, but he often spent an hour or two with the captain almost every day and for many weeks.

Apart from Winston's playfulness and fearlessness, his eyes also grabbed the captain's attention. Having owned rainbow lorikeets and seen countless others throughout the world, he had never seen one with striking red eyes like Winston's. They were that compelling he actually finished up calling him Redeye.

Even though the rainbow lorikeet is a native of Australia, Irian Jaya, Papua New Guinea, and some Pacific islands, they are today commercially bred and sold in almost every country in the world, where they have become one of the most popular birds in captivity. The captain often told the story about when he worked a ship to Izmir in Turkey. While alongside there, the shipping agent took him, the shipmaster, and his second officer ashore to have a meal at a renowned alfresco restaurant. It was a pleasant summer's day, and the place was crowded. After being ushered to a table and their orders taken, the captain looked up and could not believe what he was seeing. There was a wrinkly old man who wore a fez, plus traditional Turkish clothes, including billowing pantaloons and red shoes with outlandishly turned-up pointy toes. He was going from table to table playing a mandolin, and there, perched on the neck of his instrument, was a rainbow lorikeet that danced in time with the tune he was playing. This goes to prove they are intelligent birds and can be taught to do almost anything if they have nothing better to do.

Likewise, Winston only found his true calling after he became accidently separated from close human contact and accepted by his own kind. It was after finding his natural place in the world that his true character shone through like a moonbeam, and he no longer needed people in his life. In fact, he quickly grew wary of them in the top end because they frequently shot at them with air rifles or pelted stones at them when they were raiding their fruit trees.

There is no doubt that Winston would have passed onto his offspring many of his attributes, including his vivid red eyes. But unlike their father, they did not have to fight for their place in a flock, nor did they have to learn how to survive like he did, because the flock teaches and cares for its own. Many have the misconception that flock birds seek safety in numbers for their own survival, but this is only partially true because many of them are still taken by birds of prey, cats, human intervention, and misadventures, like colliding with obstacles when panicked into flight. The main reason why flock birds gather in great numbers is to ensure the continuum of their species.

As previously mentioned, the rainbow lorikeet has become one of the most popular birds in captivity in many parts of the world. But still, and contrary to all the readily available scientific evidence, many of these birds are given seed as their primary food source instead of commercially prepared foods especially for rainbow lorikeets. This is a travesty because their crop is not designed for hard seed and their digestive tract is short, which prevents them from deriving any substantial nutritional value from it, and this can also lead to a painful shortened life. Rainbow lorikeets held in captivity will live a lot longer for obvious reason than their counterparts in the wild if cared for properly. Yes, they will eat dry birdseed, but only if they are offered little else. Put it this way: if you found yourself locked in a small prison cell, as they are if caged, and instead of receiving your natural food each day your jailer decides through ignorance or as a cost-saving measure or convenience to give you straw to eat every day, sure, you will survive, but you will also grow very unhealthy and unhappy in a short space of time.